THE CLEVER CAT

"Poor Duchess, she just
wants to be with Richard,"
Mandy said to her dad.

"Yes, I know, love," said
Mr Hope. "But Duchess *can't*
go with him to school."

When you've enjoyed all the
Little Animal Ark books
you might enjoy two other series
about Mandy Hope, also by Lucy Daniels –
Animal Ark Pets and Animal Ark

LUCY DANIELS

The Clever Cat

Illustrated by Andy Ellis

Hodder
Children's
Books

a division of Hodder Headline Limited

Dedicated to A, C and J

Special thanks to Janey Joseph

Little Animal Ark is a trademark of Working Partners Limited
Text copyright © 2001 Working Partners Limited
Created by Working Partners Limited, London, W6 0QT
Illustrations copyright © 2001 Andy Ellis

First published in Great Britain in 2001
by Hodder Children's Books

A Catalogue record for this book is available from the
British Library

ISBN 0 340 79137 3

Printed and bound in Great Britain by
Clays Ltd, St Ives plc

The paper and board used in this paperback by Hodder Children's
Books are natural recyclable products made from wood grown in
sustainable forests. The manufacturing processes conform to the
environmental regulations of the country of origin.

Hodder Children's Books
A Division of Hodder Headline Limited
338 Euston Road, London NW1 3BH

Chapter One

"Hello, Duchess!" called Mandy Hope as she walked home from school with her dad.

The white Persian cat was sunning herself on the lawn. She slowly opened her blue eyes and had a stretch. Then she wandered over to say hello.

"I see Duchess is helping you again, Jane!" Mr Hope called to Duchess's owner, Jane Parry.

Jane was a gardener. In all the gardens she worked in, Duchess was there, keeping her company.

Jane looked up from the flowerbed she was weeding at the other end of the garden. She laughed, and waved hello. "Yes," she agreed. "But Duchess doesn't ever tire herself out or get her paws dirty. She just likes to watch – or snooze!"

Mandy ran her fingers through Duchess's long fluffy coat. The cat began to purr, and rubbed her soft face against Mandy's hand.

"She'd let you stroke her like that all day, Mandy," Jane said, smiling.

Mandy smiled back. "I wouldn't mind!" she said. "Duchess is one of the nicest cats I know."

Suddenly Jane looked a bit sad. "You're right, Mandy," she said. "Duchess is a very special cat. I'm really going to miss her." She took off her gardening gloves and came over to give her pet a cuddle.

Mandy looked at Jane in surprise. "What do you mean, Jane?" she asked.

Still holding Duchess tight to her, Jane sat down on the low garden wall. "Well," she began, "the good news is, I have a great new job – looking after rare plants in the African jungle!"

"Congratulations, Jane!" Mr Hope said, smiling broadly.

"Wow!" Mandy added. "You *are* lucky, Jane. I'd *love* to go and see all the animals in Africa!"

Jane nodded, then her shoulders slumped. "But the bad news is, I can't take my Duchess with me." She gave her cat's soft white head a kiss. "It wouldn't be safe for her."

Mandy stared at Duchess, purring happily in her owner's arms. "Oh, poor Duchess," she said. "She's really going to miss you too, Jane. And who's going to look after her?"

"I haven't found a new owner for her yet," Jane said worriedly.

Mandy looked at her father. "Could we put a notice up for Jane on the Animal Ark noticeboard, Dad?" she asked. He and Mandy's mum, Emily Hope, were vets at Animal Ark.

"Of course, love," Mr Hope said. "If Jane would like us to."

"That's a great idea," Jane said gratefully. "Thanks!"

"Glad to help," Mr Hope smiled. Then he looked at Mandy. "But now we need to scoot," he said. "We can't be late home, because Gran and Grandad are coming round for tea, to show us their holiday photos."

Mandy reached out and gave Duchess one more stroke. Then she and her dad hurried on their way.

"What should we put on the notice, Dad?" Mandy asked, as they turned into the lane that led to Animal Ark.

"Well, I think we should start with, *White Persian cat needs good home . . .*" began Mr Hope.

"*VERY FRIENDLY white Persian cat needs VERY good home . . .*" Mandy interrupted.

Mr Hope grinned. "OK," he agreed. "Then we should add Duchess's age, and Jane's telephone number. That should do it."

Mandy nodded. Then she spotted Gran and Grandad Hope through the kitchen window.

"Gran and Grandad are here already!" she cried. "I'll go and tell them about Duchess!" And she ran on ahead.

In the Animal Ark kitchen, Mandy's mum was sitting at the table with Mandy's grandparents.

They were looking at photos.

"Hi, everyone!" Mandy said as she rushed in through the door. "Guess what! Jane Parry is going to work in Africa – so Duchess needs a new home. And we have to help find her one!"

Everyone was surprised.

"Jane will hate to leave Duchess behind," said Mandy's mum.

"Yes," agreed Grandad Hope. "I often stop for a chat with Jane when I pass her working in a garden. And Duchess is never far away."

Just then, Mandy's dad came into the kitchen. After he'd poured himself a mug of tea, he fetched a sheet of paper and a pen. "Right, Mandy," he said. "Let's start helping Duchess to find her new home."

Chapter Two

"So Dad wrote a notice for the Animal Ark noticeboard," Mandy told her friends in Class 3 the following morning. They were in the playground, waiting for the bell to go. Mandy had told them all about Jane and Duchess.

"I wish I could look after her," said Peter Foster. "But I spend all my time with Timmy, now." Timmy was Peter's lively

Cairn terrier pup.

"I'd like to give her a home, too," agreed Mandy. "But Mum and Dad always say that there are already enough animals to look after at Animal Ark."

Richard Tanner looked

thoughtful. "Duchess is such a friendly cat," he said. "I'd love a cat like her. And last time I asked my mum and dad if I could have a pet, they didn't say no. They said 'soon' . . ."

Mandy's eyes widened. "Do you think that they might let you have Duchess?" she asked hopefully.

Richard smiled. "I'll ask them tonight," he promised.

"Great!" Mandy cried. She hoped that Richard's mum and dad *would* say "yes". Richard would really love Duchess, and take good care of her. And if Duchess lived with Richard, then Mandy could see the friendly Persian all the time!

That evening, the Animal Ark telephone rang.

"Can you get that, please,

Mandy?" called Emily Hope from the kitchen. "My hands are wet, and Dad's somewhere upstairs."

It was Jane Parry. "Hello, Mandy," she said. "Good news! Your notice about Duchess has worked already! Could someone take it down, please? I've found a new owner for her."

Mandy's heart sank. Richard was too late. And now, Duchess might have a new home a long way away. "OK, Jane, I'll let Mum and Dad know," she said. Then she asked, "So, where is Duchess's new home going to be?"

"Oh, I think you will be pleased, Mandy," Jane said. Mandy could hear a smile in Jane's voice. "Duchess is going to stay in Welford. She's going to live with your friend Richard Tanner and his family."

"Oh!" Mandy cried. "That's great!" Richard's mum and dad must have said "yes", and called Jane right away. "Thanks, Jane!"

Mandy put down the phone
and rushed into the kitchen.
"Guess what!" she shouted
happily. "I've
got some brilliant
news . . ."

"There's Duchess," said Mandy to
her dad, as they walked to school
one morning. The Persian cat was
scampering quickly across the
village green.

It was a few weeks later. Jane had left for her exciting new job, and Duchess was now living with Richard and his parents.

Richard had had a great time preparing for Duchess – buying her basket, food and water bowls, and toys. He'd even helped his dad to put a cat-flap in the back door.

"And look!" Mr Hope said. "There's Richard and his mum, too." He laughed. "I wonder if Duchess is following Richard, like she used to follow Jane?"

They hurried to catch up with Richard and Mrs Tanner.

"Hey, Richard!" Mandy called.

"Look who's behind you!"

Richard and his mum turned round.

"Oh, hi, Mandy," Richard said. Then he spotted his cat. "Duchess!" he cried. "What are *you* doing here?"

The Persian ran over and rubbed her face against Richard's leg, purring loudly.

Richard picked her up. "You can't come to school with me, Duchess – you'll have to play by yourself until I come home!" he said. But he was smiling.

Mandy could tell that her friend was pleased Duchess loved him so much already.

"Oh, dear!" said Mrs Tanner, sounding a little flustered. She turned to Mr Hope and said, "I'm sure this cat thinks she's a dog! She follows Richard everywhere!"

Mr Hope smiled. "You could lock the cat-flap to keep Duchess in the house when Richard leaves for school," he suggested.

Mrs Tanner nodded. "Yes," she agreed. "That's what we shall have to do." Then she looked at her watch. "Richard, you'll be late for school if we take Duchess back home now," she said worriedly.

Mandy had an idea. "I know," she said. "Why don't you walk to school with me and Dad, Richard? Then your mum can take Duchess home."

"Good idea," said Mr Hope. He stroked Duchess's fluffy head. "We don't want Richard's number one fan making him late for school," he joked.

Richard grinned, and handed a purring Duchess over to his mum.

Mrs Tanner turned to Mandy's dad. "Thanks very much," she said gratefully. Then she gave Richard a quick kiss and hurried off back home.

"Poor Duchess, she just wants to be with Richard," Mandy said to her dad as they all walked on to school. "She used to go to work with her old owner. And now she wants to go to school with her new one."

"Yes, I know, love," said Mr Hope. "But Duchess must get to know what she can and cannot do. And she *can't* go to school."

Chapter Three

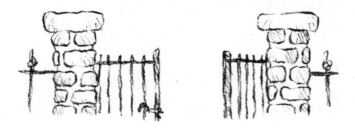

The following morning, Mandy didn't see Richard on the way to school. And he wasn't in the playground, either.

I wonder if he's ill? she thought, as she sat on the classroom carpet with the rest of Class 3. Their teacher, Miss Rushton, was taking the morning register.

"Good morning, Mandy."

"Good morning, Miss Rushton!" Mandy said, when her name was called.

"Good morning, Paul."

"Good morning, Miss Rushton!" shouted Paul Jones, who was next in the alphabet. He was the noisiest boy in Class 3.

"Ouch! My poor ears!" said

Miss Rushton. "I'm glad you're so awake, Paul, but a bit quieter next time, please."

"Sorry, Miss," Paul said, still rather loudly.

Just then, the classroom door opened.

A red-faced Richard Tanner came in. "Sorry I'm late, Miss," he muttered. "My mum burned the toast and she couldn't get the smoke alarm to stop beeping!"

Miss Rushton smiled. "Not to worry, Richard," she said. "Come and sit down."

Richard came and squeezed in next to Mandy. "I didn't even have time to say good-bye to Duchess!" he whispered.

"Never mind," Mandy said. Then she grinned, and nudged Richard with her elbow. "I can see you were in a rush," she whispered.

Richard raised his eyebrows. "Why?" he whispered back.

Trying not to laugh, Mandy pointed at Richard's school sweatshirt.

"Oh!" gasped Richard, going even redder. His sweatshirt was on back to front. Hurriedly, he pulled it over his head, then went and put it on the back of his chair.

Mandy looked around the classroom as she waited for Miss Rushton to finish the register. She noticed a big book resting against their teacher's bag.

She looked hard to see what was on the cover. Maybe the book was for storytime. Then her eyes widened. The book was called *Poems from the Ark*. And its cover was filled with all sorts of animals. In the centre was a big boat.

Mandy smiled. She knew the story of Noah's Ark. Noah built a boat called an ark, which saved lots of animals from drowning. It was one of Mandy's favourite stories. It reminded her of her mum and dad. Adam and Emily Hope saved animals too, at Animal Ark!

At last, Miss Rushton finished

the register. "Maths first, Class 3,"
she said.

The animals would have to
wait until later.

"Put your maths books away now,
please," called Miss Rushton at
the end of the lesson. "Then come
and sit down on the carpet."

"Come on, let's hurry and get near the front," Mandy said to the friends on her table. "I think Miss Rushton might read us some animal poems. I saw the book next to her bag!"

Their teacher had named Mandy's table the Green Team. And all the Greens loved animals.

When the whole class was settled, Miss Rushton picked up *Poems from the Ark,* and began to read.

Mandy thought that all the poems were great, and so were the pictures that went with them. Some of the poems were funny – and some were a bit scary!

She and Richard grinned at each other and shivered, as Miss Rushton read out *Crinkled Old Croc* . . .

Crinkled Old Croc,

Is snoozing in the river

Keeping cool, out of the sun.

But when he glides

through the water,

Looking for his dinner,

Croc's big teeth

Make everyone shiver . .

No one wants to be

In Croc's tum!

Mandy gave Richard a nudge.
"Even *I* wouldn't try to make
friends with a crocodile!" she
whispered.

Miss Rushton closed the book
and smiled. "After playtime, it will
be your turn, Class 3," she said.

"I'd like you to write a poem about being an animal. And then, for your Art lesson, I'd like you to paint an animal border around your writing. You can paint animal pictures, or patterns, like the ones in *Poems from the Ark*."

Mandy thought that sounded great! But it was going to be hard to decide which animal to be.

"We've a few minutes left," said Miss Rushton. "So everyone can get their tables ready."

Mandy's group covered their table with newspaper, and put sheets of clean white Art paper on top. Then they fetched brushes and water.

Miss Rushton squeezed bright blobs of poster paint into trays for each table. Just as she finished, the bell went for morning playtime.

"I loved those poems!" Mandy shouted to Richard, as they ran out into the noisy playground.

"Me too!" said Richard. "I can't wait to have a go myself."

The rest of the Green Team came over.

"I'm going to be a puppy, like my Timmy," said Peter Foster.

"Oh! I wanted to be a puppy!" cried Sarah Drummond. Then she smiled. "I'll be an elephant instead, then. And I'm going to paint big elephant footprints all around my poem."

"Well, I'm going to be a cat, like Duchess, of course!" said Richard. "What about you, Mandy?"

Before Mandy could answer, Gary Roberts shouted, "I know what I'm going to be: a snake – slithering all over the page!"

Mandy grinned. Gary had a pet garter snake called Gertie.

"And I'll be a tortoise, like my Toto!" said Jill Redfern.

Mandy thought hard. What should she choose? She thought of all the exciting jungle animals. "I know!" she cried. "I'm going to be a monkey! Swinging from tree to tree!"

When the bell rang for end of playtime, Miss Rushton led Class 3 back to their classroom. But when she reached the doorway, she stopped.

Then she turned round, her eyes wide. "Green Team!" she said. "What *have* you been up to during playtime?"

Mandy looked at Miss Rushton in surprise. She hadn't heard their teacher sound so strict before! What was wrong?

Richard looked at Mandy and shrugged. He looked confused too.

"We were all in the playground, talking about our animal poems, Miss," Mandy said.

"Then who has been painting on your table?" said Miss Rushton. She held the door open.

Everyone crowded in – then gasped.

On the Green table, the sheets of Art paper were covered in tracks of painted paw prints.

Chapter Four

Mandy could not believe it. "But when we went out to the playground, all the sheets of paper were blank, Miss Rushton!" she said.

"It's true, Miss!" said Paul Jones, who was in a different group. "I was the last one out, because I had forgotten my crisps. No one was in here painting when I left."

"And we've all chosen different animals," said Richard. "We wouldn't *all* paint cat paw patterns like those."

Mandy looked at the patterns more carefully. Richard was right – they *did* look like cat paw prints.

Everyone was puzzled – especially Miss Rushton! She scratched her head. Then she sighed. "OK," she said. "Let's start again. Mandy, can you fetch six clean sheets of Art paper from the cupboard for your table, please?"

The others cleared away the painted paper. Then everyone sat down to write their poems.

For the rest of the morning, Class 3 worked hard.

But Mandy kept thinking about the mystery painter. "Who do you think painted on all our paper?" she whispered to her group.

Everyone shook their heads.

Mandy got a bit stuck on her monkey poem. She nudged Peter Foster, who was quite good at writing. "What word sounds the same as 'trees', Peter?" she asked.

Peter looked up from his puppy poem. "How about sneeze?" he said.

Mandy thought for a while. Then she grinned and nodded.

"Thanks, Peter!" she said. Then she quickly wrote down her idea.

She nudged Peter again. "Do you like the last bit?" she asked.

Peter looked at what Mandy had just written, and then read it out loud . . .

> I smell jungle flowers
>
> As I swing through the trees
>
> I think flowers are pretty
>
> But they make me sneeze.

He laughed. "That's silly – but I like it!" he said.

"Very good, Mandy," said Miss Rushton, smiling, as she

read the poem over Mandy's shoulder. "You can start painting your border now, if you like."

This was the bit Mandy had been looking forward to! She picked up her brush and filled it with bright blue paint. First the monkey footprints, all around the poem. Then jungle flowers between the lines of writing.

It was going to look great!

*

Driiiinggg!

The bell went for lunchtime. All the paintings had been finished and put out to dry. The paint trays, brushes and water pots had been cleaned and put away.

But as everyone trooped out to lunch, Miss Rushton called Richard back. "It's a bit chilly out there now, Richard," she said. "You had better take your sweatshirt."

Richard nodded and turned back to grab it from the back of his chair.

But it wasn't there.

And no one else had picked it up by mistake.

"Have you searched under

the table, Richard?" Mandy
asked. She bent down to have
a look herself. And her eyes
widened.

Richard's sweatshirt *was*
under the table – and someone
was sitting on it.

"Richard! Miss Rushton!
Look!" Mandy cried.

Chapter Five

Richard and Miss Rushton both bent down to look – and gasped.

"Duchess!" cried Richard. Curled up on his sweatshirt, fast asleep, was his white Persian cat.

Richard crawled under the table, and brought out a yawning Duchess.

"Oh, my goodness!" said Miss Rushton. "Is that your cat, Richard?"

Richard nodded, going bright red.

Duchess turned to see who was holding her. When she saw it was Richard she began to purr.

"I don't know how Duchess got here, Miss," Richard said. "When I left for school this morning, I locked the cat-flap so that she couldn't follow me." He scratched his head, looking really puzzled.

Mandy reached out to stroke Duchess – and saw that one of her paw pads was bright yellow!

Gently Mandy took another of Duchess's paws in her hand and looked underneath. Red!

And another – blue!

The fourth – green!

"I think we know who painted on our table before us,

Miss!" Mandy said, grinning.

Miss Rushton laughed. "I think you're right, Mandy," she agreed. "But how did Duchess get here? That's still a mystery!"

Richard hugged his pet. "Sorry for all the trouble Duchess has caused, Miss," he said. His face was still rather red.

Miss Rushton smiled, then reached out to stroke Duchess. "Don't worry, Richard," she said. "No harm done. In fact, I think Duchess's work is very good!" she joked. "But we'd better let your mum know that Duchess has come to school today."

*

Not long afterwards, Mrs Tanner rushed in.

"Oh!" she cried. "There she is, the naughty thing! I've been looking for her all morning." She rushed over to Richard and Duchess. "When I burned the toast this morning, I opened the kitchen window to let out the smoke. But I forgot to shut it when we left for school. We were in such a hurry!"

Mrs Tanner turned to Miss Rushton. "Duchess hasn't been any trouble has she?"

Everyone was laughing as Richard told his mum what had happened.

"Duchess must have arrived here during morning playtime," Mandy guessed. "And when Richard wasn't here, she decided to do a bit of painting."

"Then she made a bed out of my sweatshirt!" Richard added.

"You certainly have a very clever cat there, Richard," Miss Rushton finished.

60

"Well! I'd better take Miss Clever Clogs home!" said Mrs Tanner. "Her paws need a good wash!"

During lunch, Mandy and Richard told their friends about Duchess's secret visit.

"So the cat paw patterns were made with real cat paws!" Jill Redfern laughed. "Clever Duchess!"

When the bell rang, everyone trooped back into the classroom.

The morning's artwork was dry. And Miss Rushton had been busy putting some of it up on the classroom wall.

Mandy went over to see whose
work their teacher had chosen.

"Look at that, Mandy!"
gasped Richard.

Mandy looked to where
Richard was pointing. There,
next to her monkey poem and
Gary's slithery snake patterns,
were a set of colourful paw prints.

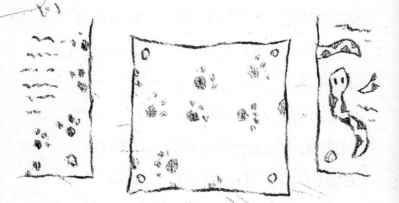

"Duchess!" she said. "Duchess's
work is on the wall!"

Beaming, Richard turned to Miss Rushton. "Thanks, Miss!" he cried.

Their teacher smiled back. "But tell Duchess that if she wants to join Class 3 again, she must paint at the same time as everyone else!"

"And do the hard writing bit, first!" Mandy joked.

Miss Rushton laughed and nodded. "Duchess is such a clever cat, it wouldn't surprise me at all!" she said.

Do you love animals? So does Mandy Hope. Join her for all sorts of animal adventures, at Animal Ark!

The Playful Puppy

Mandy thinks Timmy, Peter Foster's new puppy, is adorable . . . but he chews things he shouldn't! Can Mandy help to find Timmy a less naughty game to play?

The Curious Kitten

Shamrock is a tabby kitten, with bright green eyes and tiger stripes. When Shamrock goes outside for the very first time, he soon runs into trouble . . .

The Midnight Mouse

Mandy is helping Amy Fenton to choose just the right mouse to be her pet. But they can't think of the right name for her – until late at night, when the girls hear a strange noise in Mandy's room . . .

Look out for more titles available from Hodder Children's Books